Also by Rachael Reed

Sis
Sis 2 Blood on the Streets

Standalone
Codefendant
Codefendant
Once a Cheater
Once a Cheater
Passport Bro
What Happens in Prison
Preference
Sprinkle Sprinkle
Championship Bad
Street Exodus
Street Exodus
Street Royalty
Pawns of Power
SIS
Cartel Bloodline
Get Money Girls
Skip the Games
Til Death Do Us Part

Backpage Hustle
Link in Bio
The Virgin and The Kingpin
A Gangsta's Heart
Boosters
Can't Turn a Hoe Into a Housewife
Better you Than Me
Wig Dealer: How to Start Your wig Business
Trail Ride Blues
Demure Diva
Queen of the Carnival
Caribbean Carnival Hoe
How to Glow Up! Make 2025 Your Best Year
How to Lose 10 Pounds in a Month
What is Project 2025? The Easy to Understand Guide
What Is A Tariff
Natural Hair Growth Oil with 50 Recipes
Regrow Hair Naturally in 3 Weeks
Hustlin Through the Holidays
Same Shit Different Year

Same Shit
Different Year

Same Shit Different Year
By TBDB PUBLISHING

Chapter 1: New Year, Same Grind

The cold December air bit at Trena's cheeks as she stood on the corner, her hood pulled low over her face. Her sneakers crunched against the icy pavement, but the block was alive. Cars rolled by slow, bass rattling their windows. Junkies shuffled past, eyes hollow, palms out. Everybody was hustling, one way or another, but Trena? She'd been doing this too damn long.

Her phone buzzed in her pocket. Pulling it out, she saw Reese's name light up the screen. She sighed and swiped to answer.

"Yo, what's good?"

"You tell me, Trena," Reese's voice crackled through the line, smooth but laced with that edge that let you know he wasn't playin'. "You move that shit yet?"

"I'm workin' on it," she said, glancing down the block. A couple of dudes leaned against a busted streetlamp, talking loud and eyeing everyone who walked by. She made a mental note to keep her distance. "It's New Year's Eve, Reese. Folks spendin' money on liquor and fireworks."

Reese snorted. "Excuses, girl. You got till midnight. And don't make me call you again."

The line went dead before she could respond. Trena stuffed the phone back in her pocket, her jaw clenched. Reese always talked slick, like he owned her. And maybe, in a way, he did. He was the plug, the one who gave her the work, the one who decided if she stayed eatin' or starved.

Trena spotted a familiar face coming down the block. It was Marquise, a regular with cash to burn. She plastered on a fake smile, her hand slipping into her pocket to grab the goods.

"Yo, 'Quise," she called out, leaning against the brick wall of the bodega. "What you need tonight?"

Marquise grinned, his gold tooth catching the dim light. "What you got, Trena?

"Same as always," she said, her voice low. She pulled a small baggie from her pocket, holding it just enough for him to see. "Quick business, though. I ain't tryna stand out here all night."

Marquise handed her a crumpled wad of bills, and she slipped him the goods. Quick and clean, just like she liked it.

"Happy New Year, girl," Marquise said, already walking away.

"Yeah, you too," she muttered, stuffing the cash into her pocket.

She turned the corner and spotted her little brother, Darius, leaning against a graffiti-covered fence. At 17, he was tall and lanky, his oversized hoodie barely hanging onto his shoulders. He shouldn't have been out here, not with the way things had been heating up lately.

"D, what the hell you doin' out here?" Trena snapped, striding up to him.

"Chill, sis," Darius said, his hands up like she'd pulled a gun on him. "I was just checkin' on you. You been out here all day."

"And?" she shot back. "That don't mean you gotta be out here too. Go home, D."

Darius shook his head, his expression serious. "You workin' for Reese. That dude don't care 'bout nothin' but his money. He gon' get you hurt, Trena."

"I'm good," she said, her tone hard. "Don't worry 'bout me."

"You always say that," Darius muttered. "But you been sayin' it for years, and look where we still at."

His words stung, but she couldn't let it show. Darius didn't understand the pressure she was under, the way the streets had their claws in her. She couldn't just walk away.

"Go home," she said again, softer this time. "I'll be there later."

Darius gave her a long look before nodding and heading off. Trena watched him disappear around the corner, her chest tight. He was right. She'd been in the game too long, and it wasn't getting her anywhere.

By the time the streetlights flickered on, the block had quieted down. Trena leaned against the wall of a closed laundromat, her hands shoved deep into her pockets. Her mind drifted to the life she wanted something far from the cold nights and dirty money.

She imagined a small apartment somewhere clean, with Darius finishing school and her working a legit job. Maybe even a man who wasn't caught up in the same mess she was. But dreams like that felt as far away as the stars.

Her phone buzzed again. She groaned, expecting Reese, but it was a text from Dani, her best friend and sometimes partner-in-crime.

"Yo, you good? Heard Reese on his bully shit."

Trena typed back quickly: **"Same old. Meet me at the spot?"**

Dani replied with a thumbs-up, and Trena pushed off the wall, heading toward the small park where they always met.

Dani was already there when Trena arrived, perched on a swing and blowing smoke into the cold air. Her braids were tucked under a knit cap, and her oversized coat made her look smaller than she was.

"Yo," Dani said, exhaling a cloud of smoke. "You look stressed."

"Reese got me runnin' in circles," Trena said, sitting on the swing next to her. "He talkin' 'bout I gotta move this by midnight or else."

"Man, fuck Reese," Dani said, shaking her head. "He think he own everybody. You ever thought 'bout just...dippin'? Leavin' the block for good?"

"Every damn day," Trena admitted. "But how? He got eyes everywhere. I can't even breathe without him knowin'."

Dani nodded, her expression serious. "Still, you too smart for this shit, Trena. You could be doin' so much more."

Trena laughed bitterly. "Yeah, like what? Flippin' burgers? That ain't gon' pay rent, Dani."

"Better than gettin' caught up," Dani said. "You know Reese don't care 'bout you. Soon as you slip, he gon' replace you like it's nothin.'"

Trena didn't respond. She knew Dani was right, but the hustle was all she knew. Walking away felt like stepping off a cliff with no safety net.

As the clock inched closer to midnight, Trena's phone buzzed again. This time, it was a reminder of the life she wanted to leave behind.

"Clock's tickin', Trena. Don't make me come find you." – Reese

She stared at the message, her stomach knotting. The streets were a game she'd been playing for too long, but every move felt like it pushed her closer to checkmate.

"Same shit, different year," she muttered, slipping the phone back into her pocket.

The fireworks started in the distance, echoing like gunshots. Trena stood, her breath visible in the freezing air. Another year was starting, but for her, it felt like nothing was changing.

As Dani called out behind her, Trena walked off into the night, her mind racing with plans she wasn't sure she could pull off and dreams she wasn't sure she'd ever reach.

Chapter 2: A Deal Gone Wrong

The night was cold and quiet, the kind of quiet that made Trena's skin crawl. She parked her beat-up Honda at the edge of an empty lot, checking her phone one last time. The message from Reese had been simple: **"Drop it. No drama."**

She exhaled sharply, grabbing the small brown bag off the passenger seat. It wasn't much, just another routine drop to one of Reese's clients. Same hustle, different day. But tonight, something felt off.

The location was out of the way, a boarded-up liquor store with flickering streetlights. Trena pulled her hoodie tighter around her face as she stepped out, her sneakers crunching on broken glass. Her eyes darted around, scanning the shadows for anything or anyone that didn't belong.

"Stay calm," she muttered under her breath. "In and out."

The client was waiting by the side of the building, his face partially hidden by a fitted cap. He nodded when he saw her, his hands stuffed into the pockets of his puffy jacket.

"Yo, you got it?" he asked, his voice low.

"Yeah, I got it," Trena replied, pulling the bag from her hoodie. "But you got my bread?"

The man smirked, pulling out a roll of bills. He peeled off a few twenties, holding them out. Trena frowned, her gut screaming that something wasn't right. Still, she reached for the money.

That's when it happened.

Out of nowhere, two masked men rushed her, their footsteps silent until they were almost on top of her. One of them grabbed her arm, yanking her back, while the other pressed a cold steel barrel against her temple.

"Don't move, bitch," the man with the gun growled.

Trena froze, her heart slamming against her ribs. The client stepped back, his smirk widening as he stuffed the cash back into his pocket.

"Y'all serious right now?" Trena spat, her voice shaking with a mix of fear and fury. "This how y'all do business?"

"Shut the fuck up," the gunman snapped, shoving her to her knees. "Hand over the bag."

Her fingers tightened around the bag instinctively. "You think Reese ain't gon' find out 'bout this? Y'all dead, you hear me? Dead!"

The second man laughed, a cold, humorless sound. "Reese don't scare nobody out here. Now give it up, or I'll put one in your pretty little head."

Reluctantly, Trena released the bag, her jaw clenched so tight it ached. The first man snatched it and tore it open, confirming the product inside. Satisfied, they backed away, the gun still trained on her.

"Pleasure doin' business," the client said, tipping his hat mockingly before disappearing into the shadows with the others.

As soon as they were gone, Trena jumped to her feet, her hands shaking with adrenaline. She paced the lot, cursing under her breath, her mind racing. She couldn't go back to Reese empty-handed. The man didn't do excuses, and he damn sure didn't forgive losses.

"Fuck!" she shouted, kicking a nearby trash can. The noise echoed, but there was no one around to hear it.

She got back into her car, gripping the steering wheel tightly. Her breath came in short, angry bursts as she drove toward Reese's spot. The streets blurred past her, a mix of anger and humiliation clouding her vision.

Reese's house was lit up like a damn Christmas tree, music thumping from inside. Trena parked in the driveway, her stomach churning as she walked up to the door. She hesitated for a moment before knocking.

"Come in!" Reese's deep voice called from inside.

Trena pushed the door open, stepping into the living room. Reese was sprawled on the couch, a blunt in one hand and a bottle of Hennessy in the other. A couple of his boys sat nearby, laughing at something on TV. When Reese saw her, his smile faded.

"You look like shit," he said, sitting up. "What happened?"

Trena swallowed hard, her palms sweaty. "The drop...it got jacked."

Reese's eyes narrowed, his face darkening. "What you mean, 'jacked'? Who?"

"Couple of masked dudes," Trena explained, her voice shaky. "They was waitin'. Had a gun to my head. Took the bag and bounced."

Reese stood, his towering frame making her feel small. He tossed the blunt onto the table, his jaw tight. "And you just let 'em take it?"

"What was I supposed to do? Get shot?" Trena snapped, her frustration boiling over.

"You supposed to protect my shit!" Reese barked, his voice booming. "You think I care 'bout your excuses? That was my product, my money!"

Trena's hands curled into fists at her sides. "I told you what happened. I ain't got no reason to lie."

Reese stepped closer, his dark eyes boring into hers. "Don't matter. You lost the bag, Trena. That's on you. You got a week to pay me back, or I'm takin' it outta your ass. You hear me?"

Trena nodded stiffly, her stomach churning. "Yeah, I hear you."

"Good," Reese said, stepping back. He waved her off like she was nothing more than an annoyance. "Get outta my face."

Back in her car, Trena gripped the steering wheel, her mind racing. She had seven days to come up with the money or face whatever punishment Reese had in mind. The thought sent a chill down her spine.

The streets had always been unforgiving, but now it felt like they were closing in on her. Trena glanced at her reflection in the rearview mirror, her eyes hard and determined.

"Ain't no way I'm goin' out like this," she muttered to herself. "Not for Reese. Not for nobody."

But deep down, she knew the game had its own rules and breaking them came at a cost.

As the city lights flickered in the distance, Trena's phone buzzed again. It was a text from Dani: **"You good?"**

Trena stared at the screen, her jaw tightening. She didn't have an answer. Not yet.

But one thing was clear: the streets weren't done with her, and the clock was ticking.

Chapter 3: Streets Is Watchin'

The block had a way of turning whispers into shouts. By the time Trena stepped out of her apartment the next morning, the streets were buzzing. People leaned on stoops, smoked in tight circles, and gave her side-eyes that carried weight. The kind of looks that said her name was in their mouths before she showed up.

She kept her hood up and her head low as she walked toward the bodega. Her stomach churned as she caught pieces of conversations floating on the cold morning air.

"Yo, I heard she got robbed."

"Man, Trena too smart to get jacked. Bet she planned that shit to keep the bread."

"Reese ain't gon' let that slide. She better watch her back."

Trena's jaw clenched, her fists tightening at her sides. The streets loved drama, and her mess was their entertainment for the day. She felt the heat of their stares as she pushed into the bodega, the bell over the door jingling like it was mocking her.

Rico, the loudmouth cashier who knew everybody's business, grinned when he saw her. "Yo, Trena! Heard you had a lil' situation last night."

Trena froze mid-step, her eyes narrowing. "What you hear, Rico?"

He leaned on the counter, smirking. "Word is, you got caught slippin'. Some dudes ran up on you, took Reese's bag. That true?"

She stepped closer, her voice low and sharp. "Why you so worried 'bout my business, Rico? You tryna be the block reporter or somethin'?"

Rico laughed, throwing his hands up. "Chill, girl. Streets talkin', that's all. Folks sayin' all kinds of shit."

"Like what?" Trena demanded, her eyes flashing.

Rico's grin widened. "Like maybe you set it up yourself. That you took the stash and made it look like a robbery. I ain't sayin' I believe it, but you know how people get."

Trena slammed her hand on the counter, making him flinch. "You tell whoever talkin' to keep my name out they mouth. I don't play like that."

Rico nodded quickly, his smirk fading. "Aight, aight. Damn. I'm just sayin'."

As she left the bodega, Trena felt her blood boiling. She knew how the streets worked once your name got caught up in gossip, it spread like wildfire. And the worst part? She couldn't shake the feeling that some of that talk had Reese's ear.

By mid-afternoon, it was clear the situation wasn't dying down. Trena spotted Reese's car idling near the corner, his usual crew leaning against it. Reese wasn't in sight, but his presence was felt. The message was clear: he was watching.

As if the day couldn't get worse, Trena spotted Keisha, her loudmouthed neighbor, on her stoop with a group of girls. Keisha was mid-laugh, her voice carrying over the hum of the block.

"Girl, you hear 'bout Trena? Talkin' 'bout she got robbed. Please," Keisha said, rolling her eyes. "She too slick for that. Bet she pocketed the money and ran back cryin' to Reese like a bitch."

The laughter that followed hit Trena like a slap. She stopped in her tracks, her fists clenched, her heart racing. She wasn't the type to let shit slide, and Keisha knew better than to play with her name.

"Yo, Keisha!" Trena called out, her voice slicing through the chatter.

Keisha turned, her smirk widening. "What's good, Trena? You lookin' real stressed."

Trena crossed the street, her steps deliberate. "You got somethin' to say, say it to my face."

Keisha stood, hands on her hips. "Ain't nobody talkin' 'bout you like that. But if the shoe fit..."

Trena was in her face in seconds, the tension thick enough to cut. "You think this funny? Huh? Playin' with my name?"

"Girl, calm down," Keisha said, her voice dripping with mockery. "Ain't nobody scared of you. You just mad 'cause you sloppy."

That was it. Trena swung before she even realized what she was doing, her fist connecting with Keisha's jaw. The stoop erupted into chaos as the girls screamed, and Keisha stumbled back, grabbing at her face.

"You crazy, bitch!" Keisha yelled, lunging at Trena.

They hit the ground hard, fists flying, nails scratching, and curses filling the air. The block came alive, people rushing over to pull them apart.

"Break that shit up!" someone shouted, grabbing Trena by the arms.

Keisha's friends pulled her away, her face twisted with rage. "You done messed up now, Trena!" she screamed. "Wait till Reese hear 'bout this!"

Trena yanked free, her chest heaving. "Tell whoever you want! I ain't scared of none of y'all!"

By the time the commotion died down, Trena's hands were shaking. She wiped the blood from her lip, her heart still pounding. The crowd was dispersing, but the damage was done. Keisha wasn't just some loudmouth she had connections, and Trena knew this fight would only make things worse.

She walked back to her apartment, her mind racing. Reese's crew had definitely seen the whole thing, and if Keisha got to him first, Trena's already shaky position would crumble completely.

Later that night, Trena sat on her couch, staring at her phone. She'd tried calling Dani, but it went straight to voicemail. She felt more alone than ever, the weight of the streets pressing down on her.

Her phone buzzed, and her stomach dropped when she saw Reese's name. She hesitated before answering.

"Yeah?"

"Word is, you out here wildin'," Reese said, his tone cold. "You fightin' on the block like some hood rat? That how you clean up your mess?"

"She was runnin' her mouth," Trena said defensively. "I ain't gon' let nobody disrespect me."

"Disrespect?" Reese barked. "You think I care 'bout your pride? You out here makin' us look weak. Fix it, Trena. Or I'll fix it for you."

The line went dead, leaving Trena sitting in silence. Her chest felt tight, the walls of her apartment suddenly suffocating.

The streets weren't just watchin they were circling like vultures. And Trena was running out of moves.

As the night stretched on, Trena stared out her window, the city lights flickering in the distance. She couldn't shake the feeling that everything was spiraling out of control.

The game was changing, and the streets were making sure she stayed in check. But Trena wasn't ready to fold not yet.

She just had to figure out her next move before it was too late.

Chapter 4: Risky Moves

The sun had barely dipped below the horizon when Trena pulled up to Reese's spot. The lot was nearly empty, Reese's black Escalade parked under a flickering streetlight. Her stomach churned as she cut the engine, gripping the steering wheel tighter than necessary. She wasn't here by choice. She was here because Reese didn't give her one.

Inside, the stale smell of weed and sweat hit her like a wall. Reese sat on the couch, his gold chain catching the dim light. His boys lounged nearby, laughing and tossing cards onto a makeshift table. Reese's eyes flicked to her as she walked in, his expression hard.

"Trena," he said, leaning back and spreading his arms like a king on a throne. "Glad you decided to show up."

"I ain't got time for games, Reese," she said, crossing her arms. "What you want?"

Reese smirked, but there was no humor in it. "You owe me, remember? And I got somethin' that'll help you fix your lil'... mistake."

Her jaw clenched. "What kinda somethin'?"

He motioned to one of his guys, who tossed a small duffel bag onto the table. "Delivery. Outta town. You drop this, we cool. Simple."

Trena frowned, eyeing the bag. "Outta town? Where?"

"Don't matter," Reese said, his tone sharp. "You just do the drop. But lemme warn you don't open that bag, and don't fuck this up. You already on thin ice."

Her stomach twisted. This wasn't her usual route, and she knew better than to ask too many questions. But she didn't have much of a choice.

"Aight," she said finally, grabbing the bag. "When's the drop?"

"Now," Reese said, his smirk returning. "You already late."

The drive out was tense. Trena clutched the steering wheel, her eyes darting to the rearview mirror every few minutes. Reese's words replayed in her head like a broken record: *Don't fuck this up.* She didn't need a reminder. This wasn't just about the money this was her life on the line.

The address Reese gave her led to a rundown apartment complex on the edge of a nearby block. The kind of place where even the streetlights were too scared to work. She parked around the corner, pulling her hood up as she stepped out, the bag slung over her shoulder.

The building's entrance was dark, the glass door cracked and barely hanging on its hinges. Trena hesitated, her instincts screaming that this was a bad idea. But she pushed forward, her footsteps echoing in the narrow hallway.

Apartment 2C. That's what Reese said. She stopped in front of the door, knocking twice. It opened almost immediately, revealing a tall man with smooth dark skin and a grin that could charm the devil himself.

"You must be Reese's girl," the man said, leaning against the doorframe. "Come on in."

Trena stepped inside, her eyes quickly scanning the room. It was sparse just a couch, a table, and a few crates stacked in the corner. The man shut the door behind her, locking it with a deliberate click.

"You got a name?" Trena asked, her voice steady despite the unease gnawing at her.

"Tone," he said, flashing that grin again. "And you must be the infamous Trena. Heard a lot 'bout you."

"Yeah? Don't believe everything you hear," she shot back, dropping the bag onto the table. "That's it. You count it, I'm out."

But Tone didn't move. Instead, he crossed his arms, studying her like she was a puzzle he wanted to solve.

"Reese don't send just anybody to my side of town," he said. "You must be special."

"I'm just tryin' to get paid," she said, her tone cold. "Ain't nothin' special 'bout that."

Tone chuckled, shaking his head. "Fair enough. But you ever get tired of workin' for a dude who don't respect you? You let me know. I pay better, and I don't play games like Reese."

Her eyes narrowed. "That what this is? You tryna recruit me?"

"Nah," Tone said, holding up his hands. "Just sayin'. You got options, Trena. Don't let nobody tell you different."

She didn't respond, her jaw tightening. She didn't trust Tone, but his words lingered. Options. That was something she hadn't thought about in a long time.

As Trena made her way back to her car, her mind raced. Tone was slick, no doubt about it, but there was something about him that got under her skin. He wasn't like Reese his confidence was quieter, more calculated. Dangerous in a different way.

She slid into the driver's seat, locking the doors before starting the engine. The street was empty, but she couldn't shake the feeling that she was being watched. Her hands tightened on the wheel as she pulled away, the weight of the night settling heavy on her shoulders.

Back at her apartment, Trena sat at the kitchen table, staring at her phone. She hadn't heard from Reese since the drop, which was both a relief and a warning. No news usually meant he was waiting for something to go wrong.

Her thoughts drifted back to Tone. His charm, his money, his promise of a better deal. It was tempting, more than she wanted to admit. But crossing Reese wasn't just dangerous it was suicidal.

Her phone buzzed, snapping her out of her thoughts. It was a text from an unknown number: **"You did good tonight. Call me if you ready for real money."**

She stared at the message, her heart racing. She didn't need to guess who it was. Tone was playing a long game, and she wasn't sure if she was a pawn or a queen.

As the clock ticked toward midnight, Trena leaned back in her chair, the weight of the day pressing down on her. The streets were a game, and every move felt like it brought her closer to checkmate.

The question wasn't if she'd play it was whether she'd survive.

And as much as she hated to admit it, Tone's words echoed in her mind: *You got options.*

But in the streets, options always came with a price.

And Trena wasn't sure if she was ready to pay it.

Chapter 5: Crossing Lines

The hustle was all Trena knew, but now it was more complicated than ever. Reese still had her running his packages, but after meeting Tone, she had a second income stream and it was a whole lot better. She didn't trust either of them, but the money? That was hard to pass up.

The extra cash was like oxygen, filling her lungs and giving her a taste of what life could be if she played her cards right. Bills got paid on time, Darius finally had new sneakers, and there was even enough left to stash away. But the weight of the double hustle hung over her like a dark cloud.

Every move she made felt like walking a tightrope over a pit of snakes.

It started simple enough: a call from Tone here, a package for Reese there. She kept her routes clean and her face neutral, making sure neither man caught wind of the other.

"Yo, T," Dani said one afternoon, her voice heavy with suspicion. "You sure 'bout this? Workin' for two plugs? That's suicide."

"I ain't stupid, Dani," Trena shot back, glancing around to make sure no one was listening. They were parked in her car near the park, the windows cracked to let out the smoke from Dani's blunt. "I'm careful. Reese don't know, and Tone ain't askin' questions."

Dani gave her a look. "For now. But when they find out and they *will* it's gon' be bad. You playin' with fire, girl."

Trena exhaled sharply, leaning back in her seat. She knew Dani was right, but she couldn't stop now. Not when the money was rolling in.

"Look," Trena said finally. "I'm just tryna get ahead. I ain't tryna do this forever."

"Yeah, well, forever might come sooner than you think," Dani muttered, flicking ash out the window.

The streets were buzzing, as they always were. People noticed when someone started coming up, and Trena wasn't immune to the whispers.

"She movin' different," a guy on the corner said as she walked past.

"Yeah, money comin' in too fast. She gotta be up to somethin'."

The weight of their words pressed on her shoulders, but she kept her face straight, her steps steady. The last thing she needed was for Reese or Tone to catch wind of her juggling act.

One night, after finishing a run for Reese, she met Tone in a dimly lit parking lot. His black Charger idled next to hers, the engine purring like a predator waiting to pounce.

"You good?" he asked, leaning against the driver's door, a cigarette dangling from his lips.

"Yeah, I'm good," Trena replied, handing over the bag.

Tone studied her for a moment, his dark eyes sharp. "You been busy, huh?"

"Something like that," she said, her voice steady.

He smirked, taking a drag from his cigarette. "You know, I could put you on full-time. You wouldn't have to run around for scraps anymore."

Trena's stomach tightened, but she kept her cool. "I'm good where I'm at."

"For now," Tone said, flicking the cigarette onto the ground. "But think about it. You too smart to be takin' orders from Reese. He don't see your worth."

She didn't respond, just nodded and got back in her car. As she drove away, his words lingered. He wasn't wrong, but switching sides wasn't an option. Not yet.

As the weeks went by, the stress of the double hustle started to wear on her. Every knock at the door made her flinch, every phone call felt like a threat. She barely slept, her dreams filled with visions of Reese and Tone finding out the truth and coming for her.

Darius noticed.

"You good, sis?" he asked one night as they ate takeout on the couch.

"I'm fine," she said, avoiding his gaze.

"You don't look fine," he pressed. "You always on edge. What's goin' on?"

"Nothing you need to worry about," she snapped, harsher than she meant to.

Darius held up his hands. "Aight, chill. I'm just sayin'. You can't keep runnin' like this."

She didn't respond, shoving another fry into her mouth to avoid the conversation.

Things came to a head when Reese called her for a late-night drop.

"Yo, I need you to move this ASAP," he said, his voice tense.

"I'm on it," Trena replied, grabbing her keys.

But as she pulled up to the spot, her stomach dropped. Two of Tone's guys were standing by the entrance, their faces unreadable. She hesitated, her mind racing. If Reese found out she was here, it would be game over.

One of the men approached her car, his hand resting on his waistband.

"You lost?" he asked, his tone sharp.

"I'm here for Reese's drop," she said, keeping her voice steady.

The man's eyes narrowed. "Reese don't do business here."

Before she could respond, another car pulled up, and Reese stepped out, his face dark with anger.

"What the fuck is this?" he barked, his eyes darting between Trena and the other men.

Her heart pounded as she scrambled for an explanation. "It's not what it looks like, Reese."

"Oh, it ain't?" he shot back, stepping closer. "You tryna play me, Trena? Workin' both sides?"

The men from Tone's crew stayed silent, their hands ready at their sides.

"I ain't playin' nobody," she said, her voice shaky. "I'm just tryin' to make moves."

"Wrong answer," Reese growled.

Before things could escalate, a loud siren blared in the distance, scattering the group. Reese shot her a warning look before getting back in his car.

"This ain't over, Trena," he warned.

Back at her apartment, Trena paced the living room, her mind racing. She knew she couldn't keep this up much longer. The streets were talking, and the walls were closing in.

Her phone buzzed, and she hesitated before picking it up. It was a message from Tone: **"Watch your back. Reese ain't the only one watching."**

Her chest tightened as she stared at the screen. The game was getting dangerous, and she was running out of options.

The only question was: how far was she willing to go to survive?

Chapter 6: Dirty Tricks

The tension on the block was thick enough to choke on, and Trena felt every bit of it. Word had gotten around about her late-night runs, and the whispers were growing louder. She knew better than to expect loyalty from the streets, but the sideways glances and muttered accusations were getting harder to ignore.

Marlo was at the center of it all. Reese's right-hand man, always quick with a smug grin and quicker to point fingers. He didn't like Trena, never had. To him, she was just another hustler trying to climb too high, and he didn't trust anyone who wasn't under his boot.

"You out here movin' funny, T," Dani warned one afternoon as they sat in her car, watching the block. "You know Marlo got his eyes on you, right?"

"Yeah, I know," Trena muttered, her fingers drumming on the dashboard. "But I ain't givin' him shit to work with."

Dani shook her head, blowing out a cloud of smoke. "You think that matter? Marlo don't need proof. All he gotta do is plant a seed, and Reese'll start diggin.'"

It didn't take long for Marlo to make his move. Trena was on her way back from a drop when she saw him leaning against Reese's car, his arms crossed and his eyes fixed on her like a predator sizing up prey.

"Yo, Trena!" he called out, his voice dripping with fake friendliness. "Let me holler at you."

She hesitated, her gut telling her to keep walking, but ignoring Marlo wasn't an option. She approached slowly, her hands shoved in her jacket pockets.

"What you want, Marlo?" she asked, keeping her tone even.

"What I want?" he repeated, his grin widening. "I want to know why you out here makin' moves behind Reese's back."

Trena's eyes narrowed. "What the fuck you talkin' 'bout?"

"You know what I'm talkin' 'bout," he said, stepping closer. "Tone. Word is, you been real cozy with his crew. That true?"

"You listenin' to gossip now?" Trena shot back, her voice sharp. "I thought you was better than that."

Marlo chuckled, shaking his head. "See, that's the thing, T. I ain't gotta listen to nothin'. I see the way you move. You think you slick, but you ain't."

"Man, fuck you," Trena snapped, turning to walk away.

"You keep playin' this game, and it's gon' end bad for you," Marlo called after her. "You can't play both sides forever."

By the time Trena got back to her spot, her blood was boiling. Marlo was trying to set her up, and she knew it. But the worst part? He might actually succeed.

Her phone buzzed, and she snatched it off the counter, expecting another bullshit message. Instead, it was Reese: **"Got a drop for you. Usual spot. Be there in an hour."**

She stared at the message, her chest tightening. Something felt off. Reese never gave her this little notice, and the "usual spot" was a vacant warehouse that rarely saw action. Still, she didn't have a choice. Not showing up wasn't an option.

The warehouse was dark and eerily quiet when Trena arrived. She parked her car a block away, keeping it out of sight, and approached on foot. Her instincts screamed at her to turn around, but she pushed forward, her heart pounding in her chest.

Inside, the air was stale, and the only light came from a single overhead bulb that flickered weakly. A man stood near the center of the room, his back to her. He was tall, wearing a hoodie pulled low over his face.

"You Reese's guy?" she called out, her voice steady despite the unease crawling up her spine.

The man turned, and for a moment, she thought everything was fine. Then she heard it the sound of boots hitting concrete, too many to count. She turned just in time to see several figures emerging from the shadows, their badges glinting in the dim light.

"Police! Don't move!" one of them shouted, a flashlight blinding her.

Trena's body moved before her mind could catch up. She bolted toward the nearest exit, her heart slamming against her ribs. The sound of footsteps and shouted commands echoed behind her as she sprinted through the maze-like warehouse.

"Stop! Hands in the air!"

Trena didn't stop. She ducked behind a stack of crates, her breath coming in sharp gasps. Her mind raced as she tried to figure out her next move. Reese had set her up. There was no doubt about it now. The question was, why? Was it Marlo's doing, or was this Reese's way of testing her loyalty?

She peeked around the corner, spotting a side door partially ajar. Her chance. She bolted for it, her sneakers skidding on the concrete. The door led to an alley, and she didn't stop running until she was several blocks away.

By the time she made it back to her car, her legs were shaking, and her lungs burned. She leaned against the door, her mind spinning. She'd narrowly escaped, but the damage was done. Reese didn't trust her anymore, and now she had the cops on her back.

She climbed into the car and sat in silence for a long moment, her hands gripping the steering wheel. The streets had always been dangerous, but now they felt like a minefield, every step threatening to blow up in her face.

Her phone buzzed, and she almost didn't check it. When she finally did, her stomach dropped. It was a message from Reese: **"You good? Heard some heat was out there tonight. Stay sharp."**

She stared at the screen, her jaw tightening. He was playing games, acting like he didn't know exactly what had happened.

Trena tossed the phone onto the passenger seat and started the engine. She wasn't sure what her next move was, but one thing was clear: Reese had put her life on the line, and she wasn't about to let him do it again.

As she drove through the empty streets, her mind raced with possibilities. She could go to Tone, let him know what had happened, and make a full switch. But that came with its own risks. Reese wasn't the type to let someone walk away unscathed.

For now, all she could do was survive. But survival wasn't enough anymore.

The game was getting dirtier, and Trena knew she'd have to play just as dirty to stay in it.

The only question was, how far was she willing to go?

Chapter 7: Rivalries and Revenge

The sun was barely creeping over the skyline when Trena stepped out of her building, the cold biting at her skin. She was already running late for her first drop of the day, but as she approached her car, her pace slowed. Her stomach sank when she saw the flat tires. All four of them.

"Fuck," she hissed, kicking a chunk of ice off the curb. She didn't need to guess who was behind it. Marlo's name might as well have been written on the slashed rubber.

The block was quiet, but Trena could feel the eyes on her. The old man across the street sat on his stoop, pretending to read a newspaper, while a group of young dudes loitered on the corner, their laughter low and conspiratorial. She clenched her fists, her breath clouding in the air.

She wasn't about to let this slide.

Later that day, Trena was sitting in Tone's black Charger, the engine purring softly as they parked in a secluded lot. Tone leaned back, one arm draped over the steering wheel, his dark eyes studying her like he was trying to figure her out.

"You look stressed," he said, his voice smooth but edged with curiosity.

"Stressed don't even cover it," Trena muttered, rubbing her temples. "Marlo out here slashin' my shit, runnin' his mouth, and Reese? He actin' like it's all good as long as his money don't stop."

Tone chuckled, shaking his head. "Reese ain't never been about loyalty, Trena. He about control. And you? You too smart to be anybody's puppet."

"I ain't nobody's puppet," she snapped, glaring at him.

"Then stop actin' like one," Tone shot back, his voice calm but firm. "You got options, T. You roll with me, I'll make sure Marlo don't touch you again. And I'll pay you double what Reese throwin' at you."

She hesitated, her mind racing. The money was tempting hell, the protection was even more tempting but leaving Reese wasn't just about walking away. It was about declaring war.

"I don't know, Tone," she said finally, her voice barely above a whisper.

"Think about it," Tone said, his tone softening. "But don't take too long. The streets don't wait for nobody."

That night, Trena sat in her kitchen, her phone buzzing constantly with texts and calls from Reese. She ignored them, her mind too busy spinning scenarios of what would happen if she took Tone's offer.

The extra money could get her and Darius out of the city, maybe even out of the game for good. But Reese wouldn't just let her walk away. He'd send Marlo or worse.

Her thoughts were interrupted by a knock at the door. She froze, her pulse quickening. It was late, and she wasn't expecting anyone.

Grabbing the knife she kept in the drawer, she crept to the door and peered through the peephole. Dani stood on the other side, her arms crossed and her expression impatient.

Trena sighed, unlocking the door. "You gotta stop showin' up unannounced."

"Yeah, well, you gotta stop makin' moves without tellin' me," Dani shot back, stepping inside. "Word on the block is you thinkin' 'bout switchin' sides."

Trena's stomach twisted. "Who told you that?"

"Who you think?" Dani said, raising an eyebrow. "Marlo out here runnin' his mouth. Sayin' you tryna play Reese for a fool. You know he ain't gon' let that ride."

Trena slammed the door, her frustration boiling over. "I'm so sick of Marlo's shit! He keep pushin', and I swear to God, I'm gon' handle him myself."

"You better handle it quick," Dani said. "'Cause if Reese start believin' what Marlo sayin'...you done, T."

The next morning, Trena was back on the block, her guard up and her temper simmering. She spotted Marlo near the bodega, leaning against a car with a smirk that made her blood boil.

She stormed over, her fists clenched. "Yo, Marlo! You got somethin' to say, say it to me."

Marlo looked her up and down, his grin widening. "You mad, T? What, you don't like people knowin' the truth?"

"You don't know shit," she spat, stepping closer.

"I know you out here makin' deals with Tone," Marlo said, his voice loud enough for everyone nearby to hear. "You think Reese don't see you? You think he ain't gon' do somethin' 'bout it?"

Before she could stop herself, Trena shoved him hard, her voice shaking with rage. "You don't know what you talkin' 'bout, Marlo. Keep my name out your mouth!"

Marlo laughed, brushing off her shove like it was nothing. "You better watch yourself, T. Reese ain't as patient as me."

By the time she got home, Trena's hands were shaking. The tension was getting to her, and she could feel the walls closing in. She paced the living room, her thoughts racing.

If she stayed with Reese, she'd have to deal with Marlo's constant attacks and Reese's increasing suspicion. But if she switched to Tone, she'd be painting a target on her back.

Her phone buzzed, and she grabbed it, half-expecting another threatening text. Instead, it was a message from Tone: **"Decision time, T. I got your back if you got mine."**

She stared at the screen, her heart pounding. The streets weren't just watching anymore they were waiting.

And Trena knew that no matter what choice she made, there'd be no turning back.

Chapter 8: Blood in the Streets

The air was thick with tension as Trena walked the block, her hood pulled low and her eyes darting to every shadow. The streets had a way of whispering louder than a scream, and lately, her name had been on everyone's lips. Reese was onto her. She could feel it in the way his boys lurked, their eyes hard and their conversations cut short when she walked by.

She stopped at the corner store to grab a drink, trying to shake the feeling that she was being watched. The cashier, a wiry dude with a crooked smile, barely looked up as she handed him a crumpled five.

"Yo, Trena," he said, his voice low. "Marlo been askin' 'bout you. Said he lookin' to settle some shit."

She stiffened, her hand freezing mid-reach for her change. "What he say?"

"Just that he comin' for you," the cashier said, shrugging like it was nothing. "Just watch your back."

Trena nodded, stuffing the drink in her bag. "Thanks for the heads-up."

As she stepped back onto the street, her phone buzzed in her pocket. It was Dani.

"Yo, T, where you at?" Dani asked, her tone urgent.

"Just left the store. What's good?"

"Marlo lookin' for you, and he ain't alone," Dani said. "Reese got him out here wildin', talkin' 'bout you playin' both sides."

Trena's chest tightened, but her voice stayed steady. "Let him look. I ain't hidin'."

"T, this ain't the time to play tough," Dani snapped. "He tryin' to make an example outta you."

"Good luck with that," Trena said, ending the call.

She didn't have to wait long. As she turned the corner toward her building, she spotted Marlo leaning against a car, flanked by two of Reese's goons. His grin was wide and sharp, like a shark circling its prey.

"Yo, Trena!" Marlo called out, pushing off the car. "We need to talk."

She stopped in her tracks, her jaw tightening. "Ain't nothin' to talk about, Marlo."

"Nah, see, there is," he said, stepping closer. "Reese think you movin' funny. And me? I think he right."

Trena's fists curled at her sides. "I ain't movin' nothin' but product, like I always do. You out here tryin' to start shit for no reason."

Marlo laughed, the sound grating. "No reason? Girl, you the reason. Think you slick, huh? Think you can play Reese and Tone without nobody catchin' on?"

"I ain't playin' nobody," she snapped, her voice low and dangerous.

"Then why you so defensive?" Marlo taunted, his grin widening. "You guilty as fuck, Trena."

That was it. She stepped forward, her body tense. "You got somethin' to say, say it to my face."

Marlo took the bait, stepping into her space. "You a snake, T. And Reese don't fuck with snakes."

Before he could react, Trena swung, her fist connecting with his jaw. The impact sent him stumbling back, shock flashing across his face. His boys moved to intervene, but she was on him again, shoving him against the car.

"You wanna test me, Marlo?" she snarled, her voice shaking with rage. "Try me."

Marlo recovered quickly, shoving her off and pulling a knife from his waistband. The street around them seemed to hold its breath as the blade glinted in the dim light.

"You just made the biggest mistake of your life," Marlo hissed.

Trena didn't flinch. Her heart pounded, but her hands stayed steady as she pulled a box cutter from her pocket. "You ain't the only one strapped, Marlo."

The tension snapped like a rubber band as they circled each other, the crowd that had gathered murmuring nervously. But before either of them could make a move, the wail of a siren cut through the air.

"Cops!" someone shouted, and the crowd scattered like roaches.

Marlo glared at her, his chest heaving. "This ain't over, Trena."

She smirked, her grip on the box cutter tightening. "It never is."

By the time she got back to her apartment, her adrenaline was wearing off, replaced by a deep, simmering anger. Marlo wasn't going to stop, and Reese? He was letting it happen. She knew then that she couldn't trust him. Not anymore.

Her phone buzzed again, and this time it was Reese himself.

"We need to talk," his text read. "Now."

Trena stared at the message, her stomach churning. She didn't respond. Instead, she called Tone.

The next day, the streets erupted in chaos. Reese had put the word out that anyone caught dealing on Tone's turf would pay the price. Tone responded by hitting one of Reese's stash houses, leaving it gutted and empty.

Trena found herself caught in the crossfire, every move she made feeling like a step closer to disaster. She couldn't trust Reese, but jumping to Tone's side wasn't any safer.

Dani called her that evening, her voice frantic. "T, this shit is gettin' outta hand. Reese got his boys ridin' through Tone's block, shootin' up spots. It's a war out here."

"I know," Trena said, pacing her apartment. "And I'm in the middle of it."

"You gotta pick a side, T," Dani said. "Before they pick for you."

Trena hung up without answering. She didn't want to pick a side. She wanted out.

That night, she sat in her apartment, the distant sound of gunshots echoing through the streets. The game was spiraling out of control, and she was running out of time to figure out her next move.

Her phone buzzed again, a message from Tone: **"Stay ready. It's about to get real."**

She stared at the message, her chest tightening. The streets were bleeding, and Trena knew it was only a matter of time before that blood reached her doorstep.

The question wasn't if she'd survive it was how far she was willing to go to make it out alive.

And as much as she hated to admit it, she wasn't sure she had an answer.

Chapter 9: Family Matters

The knock at the door came hard and fast, rattling the frame like it was about to be ripped off the hinges. Trena froze in the middle of the kitchen, the knife she'd been using to cut a sandwich slipping from her hand and clattering onto the counter. The knock came again, louder this time.

"Yo, T! Open up!" The voice was sharp, familiar, and unwelcome.

Her stomach churned as she wiped her hands on her jeans and approached the door. She peeked through the peephole, her heart sinking when she saw Reese's man, Vic, standing there with a hard expression. He wasn't alone. Another one of Reese's muscle-bound lackeys stood just behind him, his arms crossed and his stance threatening.

Trena opened the door halfway, keeping her body angled to block their view inside. "What y'all want?" she asked, her voice tight.

Vic's lip curled into a smirk. "Boss sent me. Said we need to have a lil' chat."

"I ain't got nothin' to say to Reese," she said, her eyes narrowing.

Vic stepped closer, forcing her to retreat a step. "Yeah, well, he got plenty to say to you. This game you playin', T? It's over. Time to fall back in line."

"I been doin' my job," she snapped, her temper flaring. "Tell Reese to stay out my face."

"Your job?" Vic laughed, low and cold. "Your job is to follow orders, not freelance with Tone's crew. But you already knew that, right?"

She felt the walls closing in, the air growing heavy. Vic leaned in closer, his voice dropping to a menacing whisper. "Reese don't like disloyalty, T. And he damn sure don't like when people drag family into the mix."

Her chest tightened. "What you talkin' 'bout?"

Vic's smirk widened. "Your lil' brother, Darius, right? Good kid. Would be a shame if somethin' happened to him."

Rage flared in her chest, but she fought to keep her face neutral. "You threatenin' my family now?"

"Nah," Vic said, backing up with a shrug. "Just remindin' you how this works. Reese gives the orders, you follow 'em, and everybody stays happy. You don't? Well, let's just say things get messy real quick."

He turned and walked away, his lackey following close behind. Trena slammed the door shut, her hands shaking as she leaned against it. She didn't need Vic to spell it out. Reese had just crossed a line, and now her family was in the crosshairs.

Darius was sitting on the couch when she walked into the living room, headphones on and completely unaware of the storm brewing. Trena watched him for a moment, her stomach twisting with guilt. He didn't ask for this life, but now he was caught in the middle of it because of her.

"D, take those off," she said, her voice sharp.

Darius pulled off the headphones, frowning. "What's up?"

"You talk to anybody from the block today?" she asked, sitting on the arm of the couch.

"Nah, why?" he said, his tone wary.

"'Cause Reese's people been sniffin' around," she said, her voice low. "They said your name."

Darius's eyes widened. "What? Why? I don't even mess with them like that."

"I know," Trena said, running a hand through her hair. "But they tryna use you to get to me."

Darius shook his head, anger flashing in his eyes. "This some bullshit, T. You gotta get outta this."

"You think I don't know that?" she snapped, her frustration boiling over. "But it ain't that simple, D. They don't just let you walk away."

"So what you gon' do?" he asked, his voice quieter now.

Trena didn't have an answer. She sat there, staring at the floor, the weight of her decisions pressing down on her. The streets were closing in, and the more she fought, the tighter the grip became.

That night, Trena made a call she'd been avoiding. Tone picked up on the second ring, his voice smooth as always.

"Trena. To what do I owe the pleasure?"

"I need your help," she said, her voice low.

There was a pause. "Go on."

"Reese's people been threatenin' my brother," she said, pacing the small kitchen. "I need him protected."

"And you think I'm just gon' do that out the kindness of my heart?" Tone said, his tone laced with amusement.

"You said you got my back," she shot back. "Was that bullshit?"

"I meant what I said," Tone replied. "But everything come with a price, Trena. You want my protection? Then I need your loyalty. For real this time."

Her stomach twisted. She knew what he was asking, and the consequences that came with it. Switching sides wasn't just about money or protection it was about choosing a war.

"Fine," she said finally, her voice tight. "But Darius don't get touched. You hear me?"

"Consider it done," Tone said smoothly. "But don't forget, Trena you mine now."

She hung up, her chest heaving. The deal was done, and there was no going back.

The next day, Tone's guys were already watching the block, their presence subtle but unmistakable. Trena felt a small sense of relief, but it was quickly overshadowed by the growing tension. Reese wasn't going to take this lightly, and she knew the storm was just beginning.

That evening, as Trena sat on the couch with Darius, the sound of gunshots shattered the silence. They both dropped to the floor, their hearts pounding as the chaos erupted outside. Trena crawled to the window, peeking through the blinds to see two cars speeding off, leaving a spray of shattered glass and bullet casings in their wake.

The streets were on fire, and Trena knew she was at the center of it.

Her phone buzzed, and she grabbed it with shaking hands. It was a message from Tone: **"They made their move. Now it's our turn."**

Trena stared at the screen, her mind racing. The game had crossed into her personal life, and now there was no line between the hustle and her family.

She wasn't just fighting for herself anymore she was fighting to protect the people she loved.

And the streets? They didn't forgive or forget.

Chapter 10: Betrayal Unveiled

The tension in the air was thick enough to cut with a blade. Trena sat in the corner of Tone's dimly lit hideout, the faint hum of trap beats thumping in the background. The room smelled of cheap liquor and cigarette smoke, but it was the weight of the unspoken words hanging in the air that pressed down on her chest.

Tone's crew was all there, posted up, laughing, throwing dice, and acting like they weren't at war with Reese's people. Trena watched from her spot, her eyes scanning the room. Something felt off, but she couldn't put her finger on it.

She caught a glance from Marcus, one of Tone's top lieutenants. He was sitting too close to the exit, his movements too calculated. Marcus was smooth, but Trena knew smooth could also mean slippery.

After the meeting broke, Trena lingered, waiting until the room emptied out. Tone was in his usual spot, sipping Hennessy and scrolling through his phone.

"Yo, T," she called, crossing her arms as she approached him.

Tone didn't look up. "What's good?"

"I don't trust Marcus," she said, her voice low.

Tone finally looked at her, one eyebrow raised. "Marcus? Why?"

Trena glanced around, making sure no one was within earshot. "He been actin' funny. Always disappearin', comin' back with excuses. You don't think that's weird?"

Tone sighed, leaning back in his chair. "Marcus been rollin' with me for years, T. He ain't the problem."

"That's what I thought about Reese," she snapped. "Look where that got me."

Tone's jaw tightened, but he didn't argue. Instead, he nodded. "Aight. I'll look into it."

The next day, Trena followed her gut and started digging. She asked around, piecing together Marcus's movements over the past few weeks. It didn't take long to find the cracks. One of the corner boys let it slip that Marcus had been meeting with someone outside their usual territory.

By the time she had the full picture, her stomach was in knots. Marcus wasn't just acting funny he was dirty. Feeding information to Reese, setting them all up for the fall.

She didn't have time to process the betrayal. Her phone buzzed, and it was Tone.

"Yo, meet me at the warehouse. Now," he said, his tone sharp.

When Trena pulled up to the warehouse, the parking lot was eerily quiet. Her hand hovered over the handle of her door, a sinking feeling in her chest. She reached for the Glock tucked in her waistband before stepping out, keeping her movements deliberate.

Inside, the warehouse was dark, the only light coming from a few flickering overhead bulbs. Tone and his crew were gathered near the center, Marcus among them. Trena's heart raced as she approached, the weight of what she knew pressing down on her.

"Yo, Tone," she called, her voice echoing through the space.

He turned, his expression tense. "What's up?"

She glanced at Marcus, her eyes narrowing. "You tell me. Why he still here?"

The room went quiet, all eyes on Trena. Marcus's smirk faltered, replaced by a defensive glare. "What the fuck you talkin' 'bout, T?"

"You know damn well," she said, stepping closer. "You been workin' with Reese. Feedin' him our moves, settin' us up."

The crew erupted into shouts, accusations flying. Tone held up a hand, silencing them.

"That true, Marcus?" he asked, his voice deadly calm.

Marcus hesitated for a fraction of a second, but it was enough.

"Man, she lyin'," Marcus said, but his voice lacked conviction.

Tone pulled his gun, the click of the safety echoing in the silence. "You got ten seconds to tell me the truth."

Marcus held his hands up, his face pale. "Aight, aight! Look, Reese offered me money hella money. Said all I had to do was keep him in the loop. I ain't think it'd go this far."

The betrayal hit like a punch to the gut. Before Tone could react, the sound of tires screeching outside sent everyone scrambling.

The ambush was fast and brutal. Reese's people stormed the warehouse, guns blazing. Bullets tore through the air, the deafening roar of gunfire drowning out the chaos.

Trena dove behind a stack of crates, her heart pounding as she returned fire. She saw one of Tone's men go down, blood pooling around him. The scene was chaos shouts, screams, and the sickening sound of bodies hitting the ground.

"Fall back!" Tone yelled, his voice cutting through the noise.

Trena followed him, weaving through the maze of crates and machinery as Reese's people closed in. Her hand shook as she fired off another shot, the recoil jolting her arm.

She saw Marcus try to make a run for it, only to catch a bullet to the back. He went down hard, his betrayal costing him everything.

By the time they made it to the exit, the warehouse was littered with bodies. Trena's breath came in ragged gasps as she stumbled into the night, blood staining her hands and clothes.

Hours later, they regrouped at a safe house. The survivors were few, their faces grim and their eyes hollow. Tone sat at the head of the table, his jaw tight and his hands clenched into fists.

"This ain't over," he said, his voice low but filled with fury. "Reese just made it personal."

Trena sat in the corner, her mind racing. The game had always been about survival, but now it felt like a death sentence. She glanced at Tone, his face a mask of rage, and knew there was no turning back.

The streets were bleeding, and Trena was caught in the middle of a war she wasn't sure she could survive.

As the room buzzed with plans for revenge, she felt the weight of every decision she'd made pressing down on her. The question wasn't if she'd make it out alive it was how much more blood would spill before it was over.

And as much as she wanted to walk away, she knew the streets wouldn't let her go that easily.

Chapter 11: The Breaking Point

The chill in the air felt sharper than usual, smacking at Trena's face as she walked down the dimly lit block. Her mind was racing, her chest tight. The streets weren't just dangerous they were a powder keg waiting for the right spark to blow everything apart. And now? She was the one holding the match.

Her phone buzzed in her pocket, breaking her thoughts. She pulled it out, glancing at the screen. It was Reese: **"Time's up. What's it gon' be?"**

She clenched her teeth, shoving the phone back into her pocket. She didn't respond. Not yet.

Back at her apartment, she sat at the table, a notepad in front of her. Her Glock lay next to it, a silent reminder of the world she was trapped in. She scribbled down names, places, possibilities. The plan forming in her mind was dangerous, reckless even, but it was the only way she could see to end this.

She needed Reese and Tone in the same room, but not for peace. This wasn't about squashing beef it was about taking them both out before they could take her down.

The first call was to Reese.

"Yo," he answered, his voice clipped.

"We need to meet," Trena said, keeping her tone steady. "Face-to-face."

"What for?" Reese asked, suspicion lacing his words.

"I can't talk about it over the phone," she said. "It's about Tone. I got a way to end this shit once and for all."

There was a pause, then Reese chuckled. "You serious?"

"Dead serious," she said. "But we gotta meet in neutral territory. No bullshit."

"Where and when?" he asked.

The second call was to Tone.

"T, what's good?" he said, his tone casual.

"Reese wants to talk," she said, cutting straight to the point. "He say he ready to squash the beef."

Tone snorted. "You believe that?"

"Hell no," she said. "But this could be our chance to catch him slippin'. You in?"

Tone hesitated, then sighed. "Alright. But if this goes sideways, it's on you."

The meeting was set for an abandoned warehouse on the edge of town. Trena chose it for its isolation no one would hear the gunfire, no one would see the blood. She showed up early, her heart pounding as she scouted the place.

The warehouse was dark and empty, the perfect stage for the chaos to come. She positioned herself near the back, her Glock loaded and ready.

The first to arrive was Reese, flanked by two of his men. He walked in with that same swagger he always had, his eyes scanning the room.

"This better not be a setup, T," he said, his voice low and dangerous.

"It ain't," she lied, keeping her face neutral.

Moments later, Tone entered, his crew just as tense. He locked eyes with Reese, his hand hovering near his waistband.

"Alright, we all here," Trena said, stepping between them. "Let's get this over with."

The tension in the room was suffocating. Both sides stood on edge, their fingers twitching toward their weapons. Trena kept her voice steady, playing mediator while her mind raced with the next steps.

"This beef ain't makin' nobody money," she said, glancing between the two men. "Y'all keep fightin', and the only ones winnin' are the cops."

Reese smirked. "You think I'm scared of the cops?"

"Nah," Tone said, his voice sharp. "But maybe you should be scared of me."

Reese's smirk faded, his hand twitching toward his gun.

"Chill!" Trena snapped, stepping between them. "We ain't here for that."

But she knew it was only a matter of time before the fragile truce shattered.

The breaking point came faster than she expected.

Chapter 12: The Double Cross

The tension in the warehouse hit like a brick wall, thick and suffocating. The dim overhead light cast long shadows, and the faint creak of the building settling only added to the eerie stillness. Trena stood at the edge of the chaos, her Glock tucked in the waistband of her jeans, her heart pounding like a drum.

Reese and Tone faced off near the center of the room, their crews spread out like chess pieces, each side ready to move at a moment's notice. Trena could feel the weight of the moment, the unspoken challenge in the air. No one trusted anyone here, least of all her.

"You really think we here to make peace?" Reese sneered, his arms crossed as he stared down Tone. "You lost your fuckin' mind."

"Nah, I think you here 'cause you scared," Tone shot back, his voice low but steady. "You know you can't win this war."

Reese laughed, a sharp, humorless sound. "Ain't nobody scared of you, nigga. You just another corner boy thinkin' he a king."

The insult hit hard, and Tone's hand twitched toward his waistband. His crew shifted, tension rippling through them like a current. Trena held her breath, knowing it was only a matter of time before things exploded.

The first shot rang out like a thunderclap, shattering the fragile silence. No one knew who fired it, but it didn't matter. Chaos erupted as both crews pulled their weapons, bullets flying in every direction. The air filled with the deafening roar of gunfire, shouts, and the sickening thud of bodies hitting the ground.

Trena ducked behind a stack of crates, her heart racing as she scanned the room. She needed to move fast. The plan she'd been piecing together hinged on using this moment to her advantage.

She spotted Marlo near the edge of the room, his back turned as he fired at one of Tone's men. Her blood boiled at the sight of him, the memory of his smug grin and constant scheming fueling her rage.

"Time to end this," she muttered, pulling her Glock.

She moved quickly, keeping low as she made her way across the chaos. When she was close enough, she raised her gun, the cold steel steady in her hands.

"Yo, Marlo!" she shouted.

He turned, his eyes widening in surprise, but he didn't have time to react. Trena pulled the trigger, the shot echoing in her ears as Marlo stumbled back, clutching his chest. He hit the ground hard, his blood pooling beneath him.

"Fuckin' snake," she spat, stepping over him without a second glance.

Her next move was the stash. In the confusion, no one noticed as she slipped toward the corner of the warehouse where the money and drugs were piled high. Reese and Tone might have been stupid enough to walk into this trap, but Trena wasn't leaving empty-handed.

She grabbed a duffel bag and started stuffing it with stacks of cash and bricks of product, her hands moving quickly despite the shaking in her fingers. Every second felt like an eternity, the sounds of the shootout blurring together into a chaotic symphony.

Just as she zipped the bag shut, she felt a presence behind her. Spinning around, her gun raised, she came face-to-face with Reese.

"Bitch, what the fuck you think you doin'?" he snarled, blood dripping from a wound on his shoulder.

Trena didn't flinch. "Gettin' what I'm owed," she said, her voice cold.

Reese's eyes narrowed, but before he could move, another shot rang out, hitting the crate next to him. He spun around, firing back at one of Tone's men who had taken aim. Trena used the distraction to slip away, the heavy duffel slung over her shoulder.

The scene behind her was chaos. Tone was bleeding from a gash on his leg, but he was still standing, barking orders at his crew. Reese was crouched behind a crate, his face twisted in fury as he exchanged fire with anyone in his line of sight.

Trena didn't stick around to see how it ended. She slipped out a side door, her heart pounding as she ran toward her car. The cold night air hit her like a slap, but she didn't stop.

She tossed the bag into the trunk and jumped into the driver's seat, her hands trembling as she started the engine. Tires screeched as she sped away, the warehouse shrinking in the rearview mirror.

By the time she reached the motel on the outskirts of town, her adrenaline was wearing off, leaving her shaky and exhausted. She parked in the shadows, her eyes scanning the lot for any sign of trouble before grabbing the duffel and heading to her room.

Once inside, she locked the door and collapsed onto the bed, the bag resting next to her. She stared at it for a long moment, her mind racing.

She had what she needed to start over—enough money to disappear, to leave the streets and the chaos behind. But she also knew the cost.

Reese and Tone were still alive, and they wouldn't let this slide. She had crossed a line, and there was no coming back.

Her phone buzzed, and she grabbed it, half-expecting a message from one of them. Instead, it was Dani: **"Shit's crazy out here. You good?"**

Trena stared at the message, her chest tightening. She couldn't respond. Not yet.

As she sat in the dimly lit room, the duffel at her side and her Glock within arm's reach, she felt the weight of her choices pressing down on her.

The streets weren't done with her, and she wasn't sure if she was done with them.

The game was still in play, and the stakes had never been higher.

And as much as she wanted to walk away, she knew the streets wouldn't let her go that easily.

Chapter 13: New Enemies

The motel room was dark, the curtains drawn tight, blocking out even the faintest hint of daylight. Trena sat on the edge of the bed, her Glock resting on the nightstand, the duffel bag full of cash and drugs at her feet. The silence pressed down on her, heavy and suffocating. She'd been laying low for days, but the streets had a way of creeping in, no matter how far you tried to run.

Her phone buzzed again. Another text. Another reminder that she wasn't safe.

"You can't hide forever, bitch."

No name. No number. Just the promise of violence that seemed to hang in the air like a storm cloud.

Trena tossed the phone onto the bed and buried her face in her hands. The warehouse meeting had gone as bad as it could've—Reese and Tone left wounded but alive, and now they both wanted her head on a platter.

The streets were talking, louder than ever. Rumors flew like bullets.

"She set 'em both up."

"Trena made off with the bag."

"She got bodies on her now."

The whispers had turned into roars, and the block was buzzing with speculation.

Later that night, Trena slipped out of the motel and into the shadows. She kept her hood low, her hand never straying far from her Glock. She needed to make a move, but every step felt like it was taking her closer to a trap.

The bodega on 43rd was quiet when she arrived, the neon "Open" sign flickering weakly. Rico, the cashier, looked up as she stepped inside, his expression shifting from surprise to unease.

"Damn, T," he muttered, leaning on the counter. "You got some nerve showin' your face 'round here."

"I ain't here to chat, Rico," she said, her voice sharp. "You heard anything?"

Rico glanced around, lowering his voice. "People talkin'. Reese's people lookin' for you heavy, but that ain't the worst of it."

Trena frowned. "What you mean?"

"Tone got hit again," Rico said, his tone grave. "Some new crew comin' for his spots. Word is, they think you got somethin' to do with it."

Her stomach tightened. "Who?"

Rico shrugged. "Some dudes outta East Side. They ain't playin'."

As she stepped back onto the street, the weight of the situation pressed down on her like a boulder. It wasn't just Reese and Tone anymore. The chaos she'd left in her wake had opened the door for new players, and they weren't interested in talking.

Her phone buzzed again, and this time it was Dani.

"Yo, you good?" Dani's voice crackled through the line.

"Not even a lil' bit," Trena muttered, glancing over her shoulder. "What you got for me?"

"Reese's crew hit one of Tone's stash spots last night," Dani said. "It's gettin' ugly, T. They both think you the reason shit popped off."

"I ain't surprised," Trena said, her voice bitter.

"And that ain't all," Dani added. "Some new dudes been askin' 'bout you. Heard they roll deep and don't care who get caught in the crossfire."

Trena exhaled sharply, her mind racing. "Where you at?"

"Home," Dani said. "But listen, T—you gotta figure this out. You runnin' outta options."

"I know," Trena said, ending the call.

By the time Trena made it back to the motel, the sun was starting to rise, casting an orange glow over the horizon. She closed the door behind her and locked it, her exhaustion weighing heavy.

She sat on the edge of the bed, her hands trembling as she pulled the duffel bag closer. The money was supposed to be her way out, but now it felt like a curse.

Her thoughts were interrupted by a loud knock at the door. She froze, her hand instinctively reaching for her Glock.

"Who is it?" she called, her voice steady despite the fear gnawing at her gut.

"Open the door, T," a familiar voice replied.

She relaxed slightly, recognizing Dani's voice. She opened the door, her Glock still in her hand, just in case.

Dani stepped inside, her face tight with worry. "You look like shit," she said, closing the door behind her.

"Feel like it too," Trena muttered, sitting back down. "What you doin' here?"

"I couldn't sit still," Dani said, pacing the room. "This shit gettin' too real, T. You gotta make a move before they find you."

"I'm workin' on it," Trena said, her voice laced with frustration.

"Work faster," Dani snapped. "Reese and Tone ain't gon' stop till one of 'em got you, and these new dudes? They don't care who you is. They just want blood."

The conversation was cut short by the sound of tires screeching outside. Trena's heart sank as she peeked through the curtains, spotting two black SUVs pulling into the lot.

"They found me," she whispered, her voice barely audible.

Dani grabbed her arm. "We gotta go. Now."

Trena grabbed the duffel bag and her Glock, her adrenaline kicking in as they slipped out the back door. The motel's narrow alley offered some cover, but the sound of car doors slamming and voices shouting sent a chill down her spine.

"Split up," Trena said, shoving the duffel into Dani's arms. "Take the money and get somewhere safe."

"What about you?" Dani asked, her eyes wide with fear.

"I'll be fine," Trena said, forcing a smirk. "They ain't gon' catch me."

As Dani disappeared into the shadows, Trena turned the corner, her Glock at the ready. The men from the SUVs were closing in, their voices growing louder.

"You sure she here?" one of them barked.

"Yeah," another replied. "Let's sweep the lot."

Trena's heart pounded as she crouched behind a dumpster, her mind racing. She couldn't stay hidden forever, but running would only make her a target.

The sound of footsteps grew closer, and she tightened her grip on the Glock.

The streets were closing in, and Trena knew she was running out of time.

The only question was, who would find her first and whether she'd live to see another sunrise.

Chapter 14: A Temporary Haven

The bus station smelled like desperation and cheap coffee, the air thick with a mix of diesel fumes and broken dreams. Trena stood near the entrance, her hoodie pulled low over her face. Her heart pounded as she scanned the crowd, her fingers itching to grab her Glock every time someone moved too fast or looked her way too long.

Darius stood next to her, clutching a battered duffel bag stuffed with essentials. His face was tight with worry, his eyes darting toward her every few seconds like he was waiting for her to change her mind.

"Yo, T," he said softly, his voice barely cutting through the din of the station. "You sure 'bout this?"

"I ain't got no choice," Trena said, her tone clipped. She glanced at the bus schedule, her eyes locking onto the route she'd picked: somewhere far enough out of town that Reese, Tone, or anyone else wouldn't bother to look. "Y'all gotta go. It ain't safe here no more."

Darius opened his mouth to argue, but the look she shot him shut him up quick. "Take care of Ma, alright? Make sure she don't ask too many questions."

"She gon' want answers, T," Darius said, his voice heavy with doubt. "What I'm supposed to tell her?"

"Tell her it's better she don't know nothin'," Trena snapped. "Just keep her safe."

The announcement for the bus echoed over the speakers, and Trena shoved an envelope into Darius's hand. It was thick, filled with cash she'd peeled off the top of the stolen stash.

"This should hold y'all for a while," she said. "Don't spend it stupid. And don't call me unless it's an emergency."

Darius hesitated, his lips pressing into a thin line. "What about you?"

"Don't worry 'bout me," Trena said, her voice firm. "I got this."

She watched them board the bus, her chest tightening as it pulled away. The weight of what she'd done, what she was still doing, pressed down on her shoulders. She'd gotten them out, but the streets still had her locked in a chokehold.

She couldn't shake the feeling that someone was watching her. She lingered near the entrance for a moment, her eyes scanning the station. Nothing stood out, but the paranoia wouldn't let go. Pulling her hoodie tighter, she slipped out the side door and disappeared into the night.

The abandoned apartment building on the south side wasn't much, but it was quiet, out of the way. Perfect for laying low. The door to the unit creaked as she pushed it open, the smell of mildew and rot hitting her like a slap. The place had been empty for years, but it was better than the motel less obvious.

The space was bare, save for a sagging mattress in the corner and a pile of trash that hadn't been cleaned out since the last squatters left. Trena wrinkled her nose but stepped inside, locking the door behind her.

She dropped her bag on the floor and sat on the mattress, her Glock resting on her lap. The stolen duffel bag sat next to her, its weight a constant reminder of the chaos she'd unleashed.

The nights were the worst. The city didn't sleep, and neither did she. Every creak of the floorboards, every distant siren, sent her heart racing. Her hand stayed glued to the Glock, her eyes darting toward the door with every sound.

Her mind raced, replaying the events of the last few weeks on a loop. Reese's threats, Tone's promises, the gunfire at the warehouse. She'd started this game thinking she could outsmart them all, but now she wasn't so sure. The walls were closing in, and the paranoia was eating her alive.

On the third night, she heard voices outside. Her chest tightened as she crept to the window, peeking out through the broken blinds. Two figures stood near the edge of the building, their voices low. She couldn't make out what they were saying, but the way they moved, the way they glanced at the building it wasn't random.

"Shit," she muttered under her breath, gripping the Glock tighter.

She stayed by the window, watching as the figures eventually moved on, their laughter echoing faintly in the distance. But the unease didn't leave her. The streets were talking, and it was only a matter of time before someone put the pieces together.

The next day, she made a call to Dani.

"Yo," Dani answered, her tone cautious.

"I need a favor," Trena said, her voice low.

"You serious?" Dani shot back. "After all this shit, you still callin' me for favors?"

"Just listen," Trena snapped. "I need eyes on the block. Reese, Tone whoever. I need to know what they doin.'"

Dani sighed, the sound heavy with frustration. "You really tryna stay in this game, huh?"

"I ain't got no choice," Trena said. "Not till I figure out my next move."

The hours dragged as she waited for Dani's call back. Her stomach churned with a mix of fear and exhaustion. The paranoia clawed at her, every sound outside sending her into fight-or-flight mode.

When Dani finally called, her voice was tense.

"Reese got his boys out heavy," she said. "They hittin' spots, askin' questions. And Tone? He ain't lettin' up either. Word is, they both think you made off with somethin' big."

Trena closed her eyes, her chest tightening. "What else?"

"You got new problems, T," Dani said. "Some dudes from the East Side been sniffin' 'round, askin' 'bout you. They ain't friendly."

"Fuck," Trena muttered, running a hand through her hair.

"You need to get outta there," Dani said. "For real."

As night fell again, Trena sat on the mattress, the Glock resting heavy in her hands. She'd gotten her family out, but she was still trapped. The stolen money felt like a noose around her neck, tightening with every passing second.

The streets were closing in, and the temporary haven she'd found felt more like a tomb.

The question wasn't if they'd find her it was when.

And whether she'd be ready when they did.

Chapter 15: The Trap Tightens

The knock at the door came sharp and sudden, jolting Trena out of her restless thoughts. She froze, her Glock resting on the mattress beside her. Her heart slammed against her ribs as she stared at the door. No one should know she was here.

The knock came again, louder this time. "Yo, open up! This Detective Dwayne. We just need to talk."

Trena's stomach twisted. She'd heard the name before Dwayne was dirty, one of Reese's lapdogs with a badge. If he was here, it wasn't for a friendly chat. She grabbed the Glock and moved silently to the window, peeking out. A black Crown Vic sat idling in the alley, its headlights cutting through the dark.

"Trena, I know you in there," Dwayne called, his voice casual but firm. "Ain't no use hidin'. I just wanna ask you some questions."

She clenched her teeth, her mind racing. This wasn't a raid he was alone, but that didn't mean he wasn't dangerous. She slipped on her sneakers and grabbed her duffel, keeping her movements quiet. The fire escape was her only option.

Outside, the chill of the night hit her as she climbed down the creaky metal stairs. She moved quickly but carefully, her eyes darting to every shadow. The duffel weighed heavy in her hand, its contents both her lifeline and her curse.

As she reached the alley, she heard the faint sound of a door creaking open above her. Dwayne's voice followed, low and steady.

"Alright, T. You wanna play games? Let's play."

Her pulse spiked, and she broke into a run, sticking to the shadows as she darted down the alley. The sound of footsteps echoed behind her, quick and deliberate.

Trena's breath came in sharp gasps as she rounded a corner, her mind racing for an escape route. The city felt like a maze, every street and alley a potential dead end.

She spotted a chain-link fence up ahead and didn't hesitate, throwing the duffel over before climbing it.

Dwayne's voice followed her, closer now. "You really think you can outrun me, Trena? I been chasin' down fools like you for years."

She dropped to the other side, her legs burning as she pushed forward. The sound of his footsteps faded for a moment, but she knew better than to think she'd lost him.

She found refuge in an abandoned laundromat, its broken windows covered with graffiti and grime. She slipped inside, her Glock drawn as she scanned the room. The place was empty, the faint smell of mildew hanging in the air.

Trena ducked behind an old washer, her chest heaving as she tried to steady her breathing. Her mind raced, replaying the events of the night. Dwayne wasn't just here to scare her he was a hunter, and she was the prey.

Her phone buzzed in her pocket, and she pulled it out with shaking hands. A message from Dani: **"You good? Just checkin on you."**

She didn't respond. Instead, she shoved the phone back into her pocket and tightened her grip on the Glock.

The sound of footsteps outside made her stomach drop. She peeked through a crack in the door, spotting Dwayne pacing the street, his hand resting on the gun at his hip. He was taking his time, like he knew she was watching.

"You can't hide forever, T," he called out, his voice echoing through the empty street. "You know Reese don't like loose ends."

Her blood ran cold. This wasn't just about Reese anymore Dwayne was a wildcard, and wildcards were deadly.

Hours passed before she dared to move. The city had gone quiet, the usual hum of life replaced by an eerie stillness. She slipped out of the laundromat, her movements cautious and deliberate.

As she made her way through the dark streets, her paranoia grew. Every shadow felt like a threat, every sound a warning. The weight of the game pressed down on her, suffocating and inescapable.

By the time she reached another safe spot a rundown storage unit she'd scoped out earlier her body was screaming for rest. She locked the door behind her and sank to the floor, her Glock resting in her lap.

The close call with Dwayne had shaken her more than she wanted to admit. She was running out of places to hide, and the noose was tightening.

Her phone buzzed again, and she forced herself to look. Another message, this time from a unknown number: **"Tick tock, Trena. Your time's almost up."**

Her hands shook as she set the phone down, her mind spiraling. The game was closing in on her, and she was running out of moves.

The streets were unforgiving, and Trena knew that if she didn't find a way out soon, she'd be swallowed whole.

And the worst part? She wasn't sure if there was a way out at all.

Chapter 16: Same Shit, Different Year

The air was thick with the weight, heavy and suffocating. Trena sat on the hood of a beat-up Chevy parked at the edge of the lot. The night was cold, biting at her skin, but she didn't shiver. The chill didn't compare to the cold she'd felt in her chest ever since the game turned on her.

Her Glock rested in her lap, its weight a familiar comfort. A cigarette hung loosely from her lips, the smoke curling up into the night. She hadn't smoked in years, but tonight? Tonight called for it.

Her mind drifted back to that night the setup, the masked men, the sound of gunshots and screaming. She'd thought she could handle the hustle, thought she was smarter than the streets. But the streets had a way of reminding you who was in charge.

Reese. Tone. Marlo. Dani. All of them caught in the web she'd spun. Some were gone, some were still out there, licking their wounds, waiting for their shot at revenge. And her? She was alive. Free. But it didn't feel like a win.

Her phone buzzed in her pocket, pulling her out of her thoughts. She didn't have to look to know who it was. Dani had been blowing up her phone all day, checking in, asking if she was okay.

Trena ignored the message, taking another drag from her cigarette. She wasn't in the mood for talking.

Instead, she stared at the duffel bag sitting on the ground next to her. The stolen stash. Money, drugs, blood-soaked promises all crammed into one bag. It had been her ticket out, her safety net. But now? It felt like a curse.

She stood, grabbing the bag and slinging it over her shoulder. The empty lot stretched out before her, weeds poking through the cracked asphalt. At the edge, near the chain-link fence, she'd already dug a hole.

She walked slowly, each step heavy with the weight of her decision.

The sound of a bottle breaking in the distance made her pause, her heart skipping a beat. Her hand instinctively went to her Glock, her eyes scanning the shadows. But the lot was empty, save for her. The paranoia never left, even when she was alone.

"You really gon' do it, huh?" she muttered to herself, shaking her head. "'Bout damn time."

When she reached the hole, she dropped the phone and drugs in, staring at it for a long moment. It felt like burying a piece of herself a piece she wasn't sure she could live without.

"Rest in pieces, bitch," she muttered, grabbing the shovel.

The dirt felt heavier than it should have, each shovelful a struggle. Her arms burned, her chest ached, but she didn't stop. She needed this. Needed to close the chapter, to put the game behind her once and for all.

When the hole was filled, she stood back, breathing hard. The phone and drugs were gone, swallowed by the earth, but the weight in her chest remained.

She leaned on the shovel, staring at the patch of disturbed ground. The wind picked up, carrying the sounds of the city sirens, distant shouting, the hum of traffic. It was the same shit, every day, every year. But she was done.

"I'm out," she said aloud, her voice firm. "I'm fuckin' done."

The walk back to the car felt longer than it should have. She climbed onto the hood again, her Glock still in her hand, her eyes fixed on the horizon. The city stretched out before her, dark and unforgiving, but it was still home.

The night stretched on, the city alive with its usual chaos. Trena sat there, her mind racing, her heart heavy. She didn't know what tomorrow would bring, didn't know if she could outrun the enemies she'd made.

But tonight? Tonight, she was free and she was done.

And maybe that was enough.

For now.

As she climbed into the car and started the engine, the sound of gravel crunching under the tires seemed louder than it should have. She glanced at the patch of dirt one last time before driving off, the shadows swallowing her whole.

The streets weren't done with her yet.

But she wasn't done fighting, either.

And as the city loomed in the distance, Trena knew one thing for sure: the game never ended. You just learned how to play it better.

It was the year to play it different.

Chapter 17: The Streets Never Forget

The sunlight filtered through the grimy blinds of Trena's new apartment, the weak beams of light barely illuminating the cramped space. It wasn't much a one-bedroom with peeling wallpaper and a leaky faucet but it was hers. A fresh start.

Or at least, that's what she kept telling herself.

She sat at the small kitchen table, a cup of black coffee in her hand, the bitter taste doing little to wake her from the haze of exhaustion that clung to her like a second skin. The weight of the past sat heavy on her chest. Every time she closed her eyes, she saw their faces: Reese, Tone, Marlo, the people she'd left behind, and the ones she'd buried.

She'd buried more than just a phone and drug in that empty lot. She'd buried a piece of herself, the part that believed there was honor in the hustle.

Her new phone buzzed on the table, pulling her out of her thoughts.

She stared at the screen, her breath catching in her throat. The number was blocked, the message short but loaded: **"See you soon."**

Her stomach twisted. Her hand hovered over the phone, her pulse pounding in her ears.

"What the Fuck," she whispered, setting the coffee down.

The day passed in a blur of tension and paranoia. She cleaned the apartment from top to bottom, her hands scrubbing surfaces that didn't need scrubbing, just to keep herself busy. Every noise in the hallway made her jump, her Glock tucked in her waistband as she moved from room to room.

She couldn't shake the feeling that someone was watching her. The streets never forgot, and they damn sure didn't forgive.

By the time night fell, the city's hum seeped through the thin walls, the sounds of sirens and muffled arguments filling the silence. Trena sat on the edge of the couch, her Glock in her lap, her eyes fixed on the front door.

The message had rattled her, but it was more than that. It was the memories, the weight of the choices she'd made, the lives she'd taken and the bridges she'd burned. She'd tried to start over, but the streets had a way of dragging you back, no matter how far you ran.

Her phone buzzed again, and this time she grabbed it without hesitation. It was Darius.

"Yo, you good?" Darius asked, his voice sharp with concern.

Trena exhaled, leaning back against the couch. "Nah, D. I ain't good."

"What's goin' on?"

She hesitated, glancing at the Glock. "Got a message. Blocked number. Said, 'See you soon.'"

There was silence on the other end of the line, then a low curse. "Shit. You think it's Reese? Tone?"

"I don't know," Trena admitted. "Could be anybody. I got too many enemies to keep track of."

"You want me to come through?" Darius offered.

"Nah," Trena said quickly. "Ain't no point draggin' you into this. I'll handle it."

The call ended, but the unease remained. She stood and paced the small apartment, her thoughts spinning in a chaotic loop. The streets were quiet, but that was the scariest part. Quiet meant someone was planning, waiting, watching.

She checked the locks on the door for the third time, then moved to the window, peeking through the blinds. The street below was empty, save for a lone car parked at the curb.

It hadn't been there earlier.

Her chest tightened, her hand gripping the Glock.

The night stretched on, each passing hour dragging her deeper into her own paranoia. Every creak of the floorboards, every distant sound, set her nerves on edge. She knew the game wasn't over, not really.

The streets didn't let you go. They didn't give you peace. They waited, patient and unrelenting, for the right moment to pull you back in.

Sometime after midnight, a faint knock at the door shattered the fragile calm she'd managed to build.

Her breath caught, and she froze, her heart pounding in her chest.

The knock came again, louder this time.

"Yo, T," a voice called, muffled through the door.

It was Dani.

Trena exhaled sharply, tucking the Glock into her waistband before unlocking the door. Dani stepped inside, her face tight with worry.

"I finally found yo ass," Dani said, her tone sharp.

"How the fuck did you find me?," Trena muttered, closing the door and locking it again.

Dani crossed her arms, her gaze narrowing. "I got my ways. I had to make sure you were good."

"I'm fine," Trena snapped.

"You don't look fine," Dani shot back. "You look like you waitin' for a ghost to show up."

Trena sat down, her shoulders slumping. "Maybe I am."

The two of them sat in silence for a long moment, the tension thick between them.

"You think you can just walk away from this shit, don't you?" Dani said finally.

Trena didn't respond.

"Let me tell you somethin', T," Dani continued. "The streets don't forget. You might've buried old shit, but you ain't buried the game. It's still out there, waitin' for you."

"I know," Trena said quietly.

"Then what you gon' do?"

Trena looked at her, her eyes hard. "Whatever it takes to stay alive."

The hours passed, and Dani eventually left, but the unease remained. Trena sat in the dark, her Glock in her hand, her mind racing.

The message was clear.

The streets never forgot.

And neither would she.

As the first rays of sunlight crept through the blinds, Trena stood, her jaw tight, her resolve stronger than it had been in days.

If the streets wanted her, they'd have to take her.

And she wasn't going down without a fight.

The chapter closed, but the story was far from over. Trena's world was a battlefield, and the war had just begun.

Don't miss out!

Visit the website below and you can sign up to receive emails whenever Rachael Reed publishes a new book. There's no charge and no obligation.

https://books2read.com/r/B-A-WXARB-HAUKF

BOOKS 2 READ

Connecting independent readers to independent writers.

Did you love *Same Shit Different Year*? Then you should read *Hustlin Through the Holidays*[1] by Rachael Reed!

[2]

Hustlin Through the Holidays

The holidays ain't merry when you broke and fightin' to survive. Jasmine Carter ain't tryna hear no Christmas carols when eviction notices keep poppin' up, her babies cryin' 'cause they hungry, and the lights barely stay on. Desperate times call for dirty moves, so Jasmine steps into the high-stakes hustle of boosting luxury goods to keep her family afloat.

But the streets don't play fair, and Jasmine's hustle catches the wrong kind of attention. Sharice, her so-called friend, flips on her for a quick come-up, while Dwayne, a crooked ex-cop turned security guard, got his

---

1. https://books2read.com/u/3yJkOp

2. https://books2read.com/u/3yJkOp

sights set on takin' her down. He'll stop at nothin' to see Jasmine fall, even if he gotta plant fake evidence or put her in the middle of a war.

From stash house shootouts to dirty deals that go sideways, Jasmine fights to keep her freedom and protect what little she's got left. But the deeper she gets, the more she realizes the streets don't let nobody walk away clean.

Hustlin Through the Holidays is a raw and suspenseful urban tale where betrayal cuts deep, the grind never stops, and the hustle comes with a price tag you might not be ready to pay. The drama's thick, the stakes are high, and the streets? They always win.

Also by Rachael Reed

Sis

Sis 2 Blood on the Streets

Standalone

Codefendant

Codefendant

Once a Cheater

Once a Cheater

Passport Bro

What Happens in Prison

Preference

Sprinkle Sprinkle

Championship Bad

Street Exodus

Street Exodus

Street Royalty

Pawns of Power

SIS

Cartel Bloodline

Get Money Girls

Skip the Games

Til Death Do Us Part

Backpage Hustle
Link in Bio
The Virgin and The Kingpin
A Gangsta's Heart
Boosters
Can't Turn a Hoe Into a Housewife
Better you Than Me
Wig Dealer: How to Start Your wig Business
Trail Ride Blues
Demure Diva
Queen of the Carnival
Caribbean Carnival Hoe
How to Glow Up! Make 2025 Your Best Year
How to Lose 10 Pounds in a Month
What is Project 2025? The Easy to Understand Guide
What Is A Tariff
Natural Hair Growth Oil with 50 Recipes
Regrow Hair Naturally in 3 Weeks
Hustlin Through the Holidays
Same Shit Different Year